Nn Oo Pp

Qq Rr

Ss Tt Uu

Vv Ww

Xx Yy Zz

Published in the United States by Random House, Inc., New York, and simultaneously in Canada by Random House of Canada Limited, Toronto. *Library of Congress Cataloging-in-Publication Data:* Kahn, Peggy. The Wuzzles' alphabet book. SUMMARY: The inhabitants of the Land of Wuz provide a rhyming introduction to the letters from A to Z. [1. Animals—Fiction. 2. Stories in rhyme. 3. Alphabet] I. Barto, Bobbi, ill. II. Title. PZ8.3.K12425Wu 1986 [E] 85-14259 ISBN: 0-394-87876-0
Manufactured in the United States of America 1 2 3 4 5 6 7 8 9 0

The Wuzzles Alphabet Book

by Peggy Kahn
illustrated by Bobbi Barto

Random House 🏠 New York

Alphabet Time

The Wuzzles are ready
for alphabet time.
While they play
with the letters,
they'll tell you a rhyme.
They're here to invite you
to ABC fun.
You'll know letters better
before you are done.

A a

A is for apple,
so shiny and red!
Rhinokey is balancing
one on his head.
Butterbear's apples
grow on a tree.
How many apples
do you see?

Bb

B is for balls
to bounce or to throw,
to hit with a bat
or to mold out of snow,
to toss in the air
or to roll on the ground!
Balls never are square—
They're almost all round!

Cc

C is for carrots
and cabbage
and candy.
C is for cupcakes
the Wuzzles keep handy.
C is for cookies.
Don't they look yummy?
Hoppopotamus pops them
right into her tummy!

Dd

D is for doors
Wuzzles open and close.
Be careful, Rhinokey!
Watch out for your nose!
Knock, knock on a door
to say that you're there.
Hold open a door
to show that you care!

Ee

E is for elves
you rarely will see.
Can you find a few
on the branch of this tree?

Ff

F is for flowers
that grow toward the sun.
Butterbear greets them
one by one.
She gives them a drink
of water each day,
and the flowers are happy
she treats them that way!

Gg

G is for the ghost
that on Halloween night
might give a Wuzzle
a bit of a fright.
Kids dressed in costumes
shout "Trick or treat!"
Their bags are soon full
of goodies to eat!

Hh

H is for hats—
any shape, any size!
A hat for a party
or to hide a surprise!
A hat with a feather!
A hat with a bow!
A hat to wear fishing!
A hat for the snow!
A hat for a cook!
A hat for a clown!
A hat for the country!
A hat for the town!

Ii

I is for ice cream
on cones or in dishes,
which all of the Wuzzles
agree tastes delicious!
Hooray for *all* ice cream!
A wonderful treat!
Was there ever
anything better to eat?
As for ice cream sodas,
the Wuzzles all think
there never was
anything better to drink!

J j

J is for junk
Eleroo just adores
to put in his pocket
or store out of doors.
A toy that is broken,
a small piece of string,
a bike with one wheel—
he keeps everything!

Kk

K is for kids!
Girls and boys—
boys and girls—
with pigtails and Afros,
with crew cuts and curls!
Thin kids and fat kids,
small kids and tall.
The Wuzzles love *all* kids—
A-L-L . . . *all!*

L l

L is for lamps
the Wuzzles might light
to brighten the darkness
that comes with the night.

Mm

M is for the moon
that sails overhead.

Nn

N is for nighties
for wearing to bed.

Oo

O is for ornaments
to hang on the tree.
Christmas is such fun,
the Wuzzles agree.

Pp

P is for packages
with ribbons and bows
and presents inside them,
as everyone knows.

Q q

Q is for a queen
who is wearing a crown
with sparkling jewels
and a long velvet gown.

Rr

R is for roller skates
Rhinokey wears,
and for rubber raincoats
and rocking chairs.

Ss

S is for a snuzzle,
a cuddlesome hug,
delivered by Wuzzles
to make you feel snug.
If you're feeling tired
or grumpy or blue,
a Wuzzle will give
a good snuzzle to you!

Tt

T is for trumpets—
tubas—trombones—
and the ting-a-ling-ling
of ten telephones!
The rattle-tat-tat
of a tambourine—
things that are heard
and not only seen!

Uu

U is for umbrellas—
blue, yellow, and red—
that keep falling raindrops
off all Wuzzles' heads!
When they go to the beach
and the sun's very strong,
the Wuzzles might take
beach umbrellas along!

V v

V is for violets
to pick on spring days,
which make a bouquet
to put in a vase.
The Wuzzles need **V**
to spell violin.
Rhinokey will play.
Let the music begin!

W w

W is for Wuzzles
and the wings Wuzzles wear
to give them a lift
when they take to the air.
Wheels on a wagon
and wheels on a bike
are **W** words
the Wuzzles all like!

Xx

X is for xylophone
to plink-plank a song.

Yy

Y is for yo-yos
with strings that are long.

Zz

Z is for zipper
to zip up your clothes.
And **Z** ends the alphabet,
as each Wuzzle knows!

Aa Bb Cc

Dd Ee

Ff Gg Hh

Ii Jj Kk

Ll Mm